Look . . .

From behind, you'll find

it looks like a horse, of course.

But it was born with a horn on its head . . .

SO WHAT?

The Land of Sweet Dreams

Sweet
CYPRESS HILL

The Lathering
LAKE OF
LUSHNESS

The Friendly
Forest of
HEARTS

The Wonderful
WASHPLACE

The Super Sunny
SUNNY SLOPE

The Waterfall of
WHOOSHING
WISHES

The Pools of
PINKAPOO
PLANTS

The
TOWER
of Terrible
TROUBLES

N

W        E

S

To NOWHERE

A TEMPLAR BOOK

Published in the UK in 2021 by Templar Books,
an imprint of Bonnier Books UK,
The Plaza, 535 King's Road, London, SW10 0SZ
www.templarco.co.uk
www.bonnierbooks.co.uk

First edition 2019

1 3 5 7 9 10 8 6 4 2

Written by Marc-Uwe Kling
Illustrated by Astrid Henn

Original edition:
Edited by Frank Kuhne and Marlen Bialek
Production: Bettina Oguamanam

English language edition:
Translated by Boris Löbsack
Edited by Lydia Watson and Katie Haworth
Designed by Olivia Cook
Production by Neil Randles

Printed in Poland

Marc-Uwe Kling    Astrid Henn

# The Unicorn that Said NO

templar
books

In the Forest of Hearts where the unicorns roam,
there are candyfloss clouds – it's a hip-happy home.

It lies in the magical Land of Sweet Dreams,
where the pink fluffy rocks taste of strawberry creams.

No one eats porridge or spinach or bread,
they have biscuits and jam tarts for breakfast instead.

It's a wonderful land! It's happy and free!
And the unicorns here are as nice as can be.

But then one joyful and glittering day,
a new little unicorn came out to play.

Where did it come from? Nobody knows.
Did it hatch from an egg, or bloom from a rose?

## An egg? Wait. What the heck?

Do unicorns lay eggs? I can't tell you that.
Let's say a magician pulled it out of a hat.

Ha ha, very funny.

## Anyway. . .

It was so cute its parents were glowing with pride.
"It fits in our family! It's perfect!" they cried.

From its head to its tail to its horn to its feet,
it was sweepity, swoopity, swappity sweet!

But it felt out of place as it started to grow.
It wasn't sure why – it just didn't know.

So it didn't speak much, except to say:

NO!

A great word, it thought,
with a magic of sorts:

to baths,

to food,

to school,

to sports.

It said NO so often its aunt was appalled.
"Not uni- but uNOcorn, you should be called!"

"For our child to be happy," its dad said one day,
"We must give it *more* snuggles and cuddles and play!"

So he said to the child, "Why don't we hop over
to Sweet Cypress Hill to eat sugary clover?"

The uNOcorn scratched its head with its toe,
then it turned round and – surprise! – it said:

NO!

"All right," said its mum. "Then how about this?
I know three little cherubs who'll give you a kiss!

Their laughter is tuneful and never too loud,
and they live in the fluffiest, snuggliest cloud!

Shall we pop up to see them and give it a go?"
The uNOcorn thought . . . and then it said:

NO!

The uNOcorn's brother, while blowing a kiss,
said, "Don't worry folks, let *me* handle this!

Let's visit the fairies who daintily dance
for the cute little gnomes in the pinkapoo plants.

What do you think? Will you come with your bro?"
The uNOcorn scowled and quite firmly said:

NO!

Unwanted suggestions then came by the dozen,
including this one, from the uNOcorn's COWsin:

"Why don't we play in the waterfall's bubbles?
Splashing about, you'll forget all your troubles!

It will be a-MOO-zing! Come with me, let's go!"
But the unicorn shouted:

NO!
NO!
NO!
NO!
NO!

The uNOcorn's stubbornness caused great displeasure.

Well what do you want?

they all asked it together.

"We've pretty much had enough of your tone!"
The uNOcorn answered, "Just leave me ALONE!"

"But why?" asked its grandpa. "Why make such a fuss?
Why can't you be hip-hoppy-happy like us?"

The uNOcorn said, "I can't smile *all* of the time!

And I also don't like that every sentence here is a . . . stupid poem."

I'VE HAD IT UP TO HERE!

"Uh, yes. Oh well," said the others. "Okay."

**"BYE NOW,"** said the uNOcorn.

For the rest of the day,
the uNOcorn played in the mud.

It ate soggy apples until it was sick,
and it chased cute little kittens up trees.

That put the uNOcorn in quite a good
mood. It also made it thirsty, so it went
down to the river for a drink.

Miaaoww!

At the river, it met a raccoon having a wash.
"Do you want to wash too?" the raccoon asked.

The uNOcorn grumbled, "Er, yuck. No way!
I don't want a bath today."

And then it got annoyed because it had accidentally rhymed.
But the raccoon didn't seem to have heard.

"Pardon me?"

"You must be hard of hearing," snorted the uNOcorn.

"You'll have to talk louder," said the raccoon. "I'm hard of hearing."

"Thought so," said the uNOcorn.

"Huh?"

"Great," muttered the uNOcorn, "a HUHcoon . . ."

"Huh?"

"DO YOU ACTUALLY HEAR BAD OR ARE YOU
JUST NOT REALLY LISTENING?" shouted the uNOcorn.

"A bit of both," said the HUHcoon.

"I see."

"Where are you going, anyway?"
the HUHcoon asked.

"Nowhere," said the uNOcorn.

"Huh?"

"NOWHERE!"

"Oh good," said the HUHcoon.
"I was just about to go there myself.
Can I come with you?"

It was all ready to go.
The uNOcorn said . . .

OK, WHATEVER.

So, they trotted off together to Nowhere.

It wasn't long before they came to a small hill,
and at the top was a watchdog lying in the sun.

"Move over," said the uNOcorn. "I want to lie in the sun, too."

So what?

asked the watchdog.

"So **make way**, or you'll have to fight me!" said the uNOcorn,
and scraped its front hoof on the ground threateningly.

"So what?" said the watchdog.

"So if you're a watchdog, you should probably be watching something!"

"So what?" asked the watchdog.

"Shouldn't you at least be in dog training school right now?"

"So what?"

"Besides, you stink."

"So what?"

"So you should take a bath! Doesn't your family expect
you to do baths and school and food and sports?"

"So what?"

HA!

cried the uNOcorn.
"You're a SOWHATchdog."

"And can I ask who YOU are?" asked the SOWHATchdog.

"No!"

"Oh, so you don't do being friendly?"

"No, I don't!"

"Let me guess. Are you a DON'Tkey?"

The uNOcorn was outraged. "Do donkeys have such a beautiful horn?"

The SOWHATchdog grinned. "You're the uNOcorn."

The uNOcorn nodded proudly. "Yes!"

The SOWHATchdog said:

We could still be friends though.

And the uNOcorn replied . . .

YEAH, WHY NOT.

Huh?

asked the HUHcoon.

Together, they continued their journey to Nowhere.

Before long, they arrived at a big tower. The tower had a princess locked up at the top. There is always a princess locked up in these kinds of towers.

"Help me!" she cried.

"No!" said the uNOcorn.

# Yes!

said the Princess crossly. "I'm locked up!"

"So what?" called the SOWHATchdog. "It's not our job to rescue total-stranger princesses!"

The three of them stood in front of the tower and made no attempt to save the princess.

"You have to help me!" she shouted angrily.

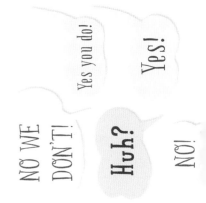

NO WE DON'T!

Yes you do!

Huh?

Yes!

NO!

Yes! You are my subjects!

So what?

Huh?

Yes!

"That must be the Prince **YES**," said the uNOcorn.

"That's right!" she said. "My father locked me up in here because I always talk back."

"*No!*"

"*Yes!*"

"Hey, I think the princess is locked away up there," said the HUHcoon.

"**So what?**" said the SOWHATchdog.

"Aren't we going to help her?" asked the HUHcoon.

"No."

"**Yes!**" cried the princess from above.

"Oh, all right," said the uNOcorn finally.

Woof!

The SOWHATchdog gave a loud bark, which made the guard run away.
He dropped the key, of course. Guards like that always drop the key.

The HUHcoon grabbed the key and climbed up a vine
to the PrinceYES. Now she could unlock the door herself.

But once she got downstairs, the stupid wooden
door was totally jammed.

The uNOcorn lowered
its horn and charged.

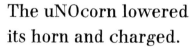

CRASH!

The door shattered into pieces.
And bam: the PrinceYES was free.

The first thing she said was: "Awwwwww!
You are such an adorable unicorn!
Will you give me a ride?"

NO!

Yes!

"Only if you give **ME** a ride first," said the uNOcorn.

And so the PrincYES gave the uNOcorn a piggyback.
You didn't see that coming, huh?

So anyway, the uNOcorn and the PrinceYES could have really endless conversations. They went something like this:

NO! Yes!

NO! Yes!

NO! Yes!

NO! Yes!

NO! Yes!

NO! Yes!

NO! Yes!

Yes!

Huh? Yes!

NO! Yes!

NO!

Sometimes the HUHcoon and the SOWHATchdog would join in, and then it would sound something like this:

So now the uNOcorn, the SOWHATchdog,
the HUHcoon and the PrinceYES hang out all the time.
Because even being stubborn is more fun together.

And if someone tells them, "But you can't be so stubborn all the time!"
the PrinceYES says, "Yes, we can!"

Once in a while the uNOcorn also says, "So what?"
and the SOWHATchdog says, "No!"

They do that to confuse the other animals in the Forest of Hearts.

The HUHcoon usually just says, "Huh?" He's hard of hearing.
Or maybe he just doesn't really listen. A bit of both.

Occasionally they're even in a good mood.
Everyone needs that now and again.

They even join the unicorn family sometimes,
but they always insist that not everything rhymes.

(And they refuse to eat their greens . . .)

YUCK!

Well. That was the story of the uNOcorn and its friends.

I asked the uNOcorn if the story needed a moral, but of course it said, "No!"

I explained that many adults think that children's books should have a moral and therefore be pedagogically valuable. But the SOWHATchdog said: "So what?" and the HUHcoon wasn't really listening.

If you would like the story to have a moral, just make one up.

Maybe you'd like to invent stories about other animals (with or without a moral). Have you ever heard of any of these creatures? Can you think of even more?

The Huguar

The Habbit

The Snobster

The Battlesnake

*The* Humblebee

*The* Tipmunk

*The* Lie-on

*The* Nicebear

*The* Frownfish